(#-8)

JACK AND THE MEANSTALK

BY
BRIAN
AND
REBECCA
WILDSMITH

ALFRED A. KNOPF NEW YORK

Professor Jack was a scientist, but his first love was his garden. He spent all his spare time growing vegetables, and nothing pleased him more than a fresh carrot or a ripe tomato.

Professor Jack was also a very impatient man. Crops that didn't sprout quickly enough annoyed him. And so he decided to invent a way to make them grow faster.

Professor Jack disappeared into his laboratory and began experimenting. He mixed up a batch of chemicals and poured them over the seeds he'd collected from his garden.

He laughed, picturing plants that would be the envy of every gardener he knew. "Now we shall see how fast my vegetables grow!" he said to himself.

Early the next morning, Professor Jack woke to a loud crash. He ran outside and saw that his experiment had worked better than he could have ever dreamed. The villagers gathered quickly, and by midday, two television crews had arrived to witness the extraordinary plant.

As the plant continued to grow, so did the news of its
incredible size. All those who set eyes upon it were bewildered.

By now the plant had burst
through the ozone layer, and its thousands
of leaves were blocking out the sunlight. The earth's
governments sent fighter planes to try to shoot it down.
People became afraid. And still the plant grew.

Meanwhile, the plant's roots bulged out of the soil,
erupting throughout the countryside, destroying towns,
villages, and everything in its way.

But the worst was yet to come. A satellite sent back pictures of a space monster that appeared to be climbing down the giant plant toward the earth. Now people were truly terrified. No one knew what to do.

The animals were frightened too. Their homes were
being destroyed, and soon they would have nowhere to live,
and nothing to eat or drink. Badger called an emergency meeting.

"We must get to the root of the problem," said Fox.
"The roots! There's the answer," Owl cried. "We must eat
through the roots of the giant plant and kill it once and for all."

Foxes, rabbits, moles, and all who could burrow
waited for Badger's word of command. At Badger's signal,
they started to dig and gnaw and bite through the roots
of the plant.

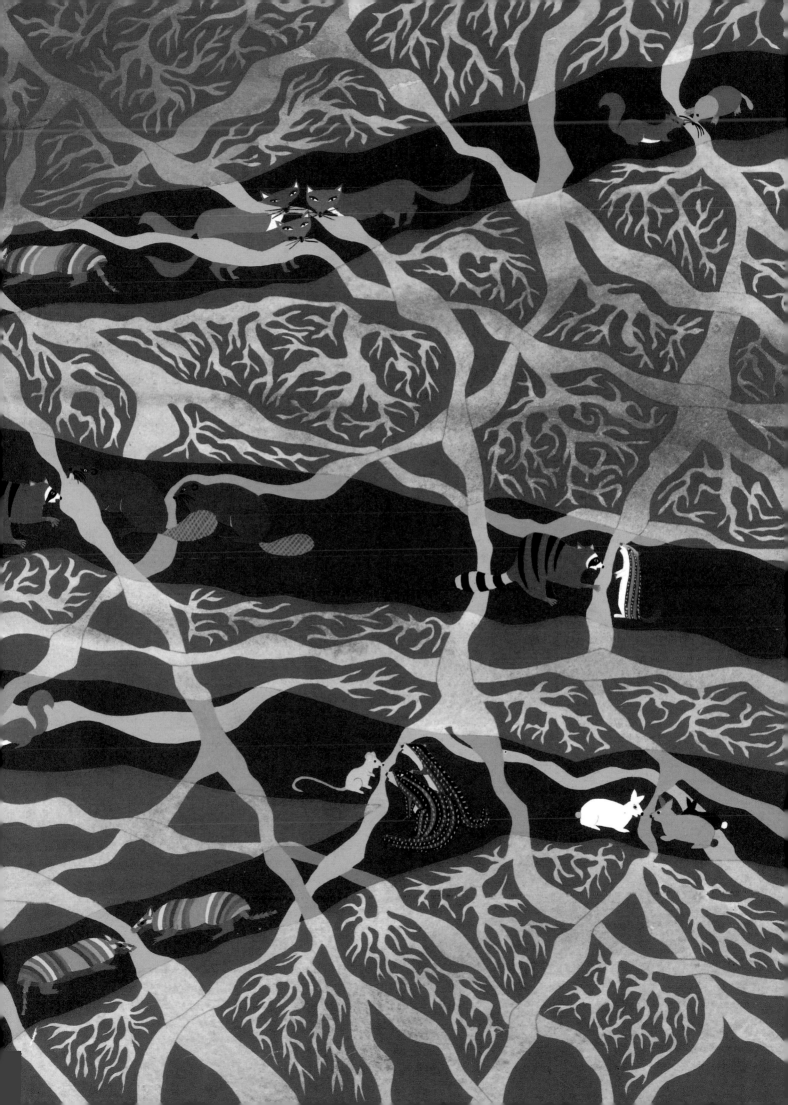

Day after day, night after night, the burrowing animals tore at the roots with their teeth and claws. And finally the giant plant, with no nourishment from the soil, weakened. When it died, it snapped into pieces, which scattered into space, taking the monster with them.

In time, the countryside recovered. Towns and villages
were rebuilt, and people and animals went on with their lives.
Professor Jack repaired his house and planted a new
garden. But this time, he let nature take its course.

For Clare, Anna, and Simon

THIS IS A BORZOI BOOK PUBLISHED BY ALFRED A. KNOPF, INC.

Text and illustrations copyright © 1994 by Brian and Rebecca Wildsmith
All rights reserved under International and Pan-American Copyright Conventions.
Published in the United States of America by Alfred A. Knopf, Inc., New York.
Originally published in Great Britain by Oxford University Press in 1994.
Distributed by Random House, Inc., New York.

Library of Congress Cataloging-in-Publication Data
Wildsmith, Brian. Jack and the meanstalk / by Brian and Rebecca Wildsmith. p. cm.
Summary: When a scientist's experiment to grow bigger vegetables threatens the
whole Earth the animals find a way to save the day.
ISBN 0-679-85810-5 (trade)   ISBN 0-679-95810-X (lib. bdg.)
[1. Science fiction. 2. Plants—Fiction. 3. Animals—Fiction.]
I. Wildsmith, Rebecca, ill. II. Title PZ7.W647Jac 1994 [E]—dc20 93-30374

Manufactured in Hong Kong 10 9 8 7 6 5 4 3 2 1